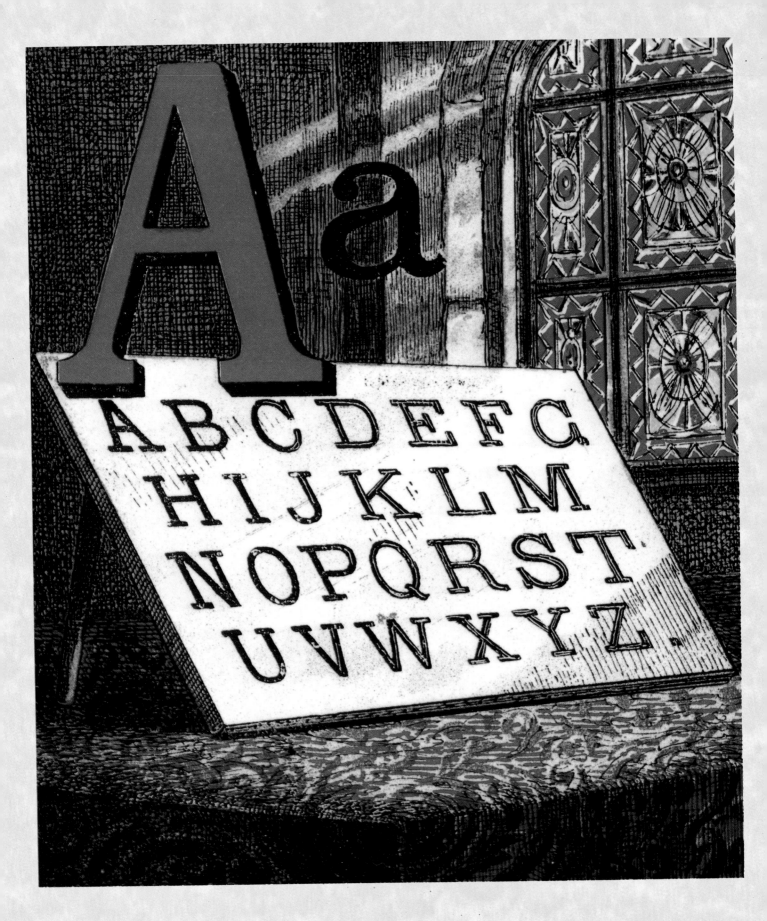

AN OLD FASHIONED
NURSERY
ALPHABET

FROM AUNT LOUISA'S TOY SERIES

Bracken Books
LONDON

Published by Bracken Books
a division of Bestseller Publications Limited,
Princess House, 50 Eastcastle Street,
London W1N 7AP

Copyright © Bracken Books 1987.

ISBN 1 85170-111-7

Printed and bound by Times Printers, Singapore.

Badger

A is an Artist, who copies so well,
That likeness from sitter one scarcely
    can tell

B is a Blacksmith, who hammers away
With a clang and a clatter throughout
    the whole day

C is a Cobbler, who sticks to his last,
His work strong and neat, though he
    stitches so fast

D is a Dressmaker, whose work seems
    but play,
For she's making a dress for her own
    wedding day

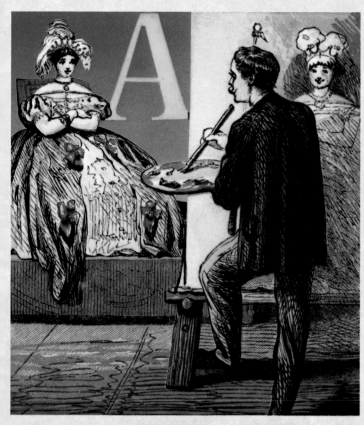

Able	Ale		
Ace	All		
Ache	Ally		
Acid	Alms		
Acre	Alps		
Act	Amen	Arch	
Add	Amid	Ark	
Aft	Ant	Art	
Age	Any	Ash	Awe
Aid	Apse	Ask	Awl
Aim	Apt	Asp	Axis
Air	Arc	Away	Axle

Ape

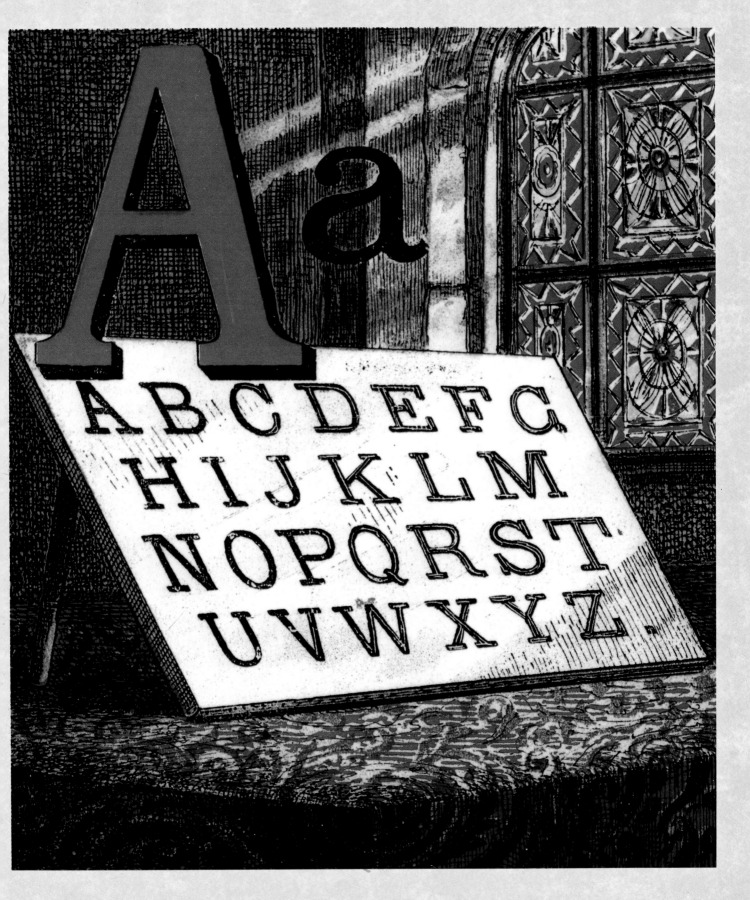

A for the Alphabet, A, B, C

Baby	Bean	Big	Boot
Bag	Beat	Bin	Both
Bake	Bee	Bird	Bow
Bald	Beef	Bit	Box
Ball	Bell	Blow	Boy
Band	Bet	Blue	Brig
Bank	Bid	Boat	Brim
Bar			
Barn			
Base			
Bath			
Bay			

Bear

B for the Book that was given to me

Camel

City

Clam

Clap

Clay

Clip

Coal

Cab	Can	Cask	Coat
Cake	Cane	Cat	Coax
Calf	Cap	Cave	Cob
Call	Card	Cell	Cod
Calm	Cart	Cent	Cog
Camp	Case	Chin	Coin

C for the Corn that stands in the stack

Dab	Darn	Deed	Dip
Dad	Date	Deep	Dish
Dale	Day	Den	Dock
Dam	Deal	Desk	Don
Dame	Debt	Dial	Done
Damp	Deck	Dig	Door
			Dot
			Dove
			Down
			Dray
			Drum
			Dry

Dog

D for the Donkey with cross on his back

A a
B b
C c
D d

A Apple-stall. **B** Bazaar.

C Cabs. **D** Dustman.

A a
B b
C c
D d

A Acorn.   B Barn.

C Cows.   D Ducks.

E an Engineer, files and hammers away,
Moulding iron and brass as though they
were clay

F is a Flower-girl, fair and modest as
well,
Who with a sweet voice cries "Flowers
to sell"

G is a Gardener, of such skill and care
That no flowers or plants with his can
compare

H is a Hatter, who alters the brims
And crowns of his hats, to suit fashion's
whims

Each

Ear

Earl

East

Easy

Eat

Elephant

Ebb	Ego	Emu	Even
Echo	Elf	End	Ever
Edge	Elk	Epic	Evil
Edit	Elm	Era	Ewe
Eel	Else	Espy	Exert
Egg	Empt	Etch	Exit

E for the Engine that's lighted with coal

Face	Feet	Fire	Foot
Fact	Fen	Fish	Fort
Fade	Fern	Fit	Fray
Fair	Fife	Flag	Fret
Fall	Fig	Flap	Frog
Fan	File	Fly	Fry
Fang	Find	Foal	Fuel
Far	Fir	Fog	Full
Fare			
Farm			
Fat			
Fate			

Fox

F for the Funnel that puffs out the smoke

Gag	Get	Gown	Gray
Gain	Gibe	Gram	Grin
Gale	Gift		Grip
Gall	Gig		Grit
Game	Girl		
Gap	Glad		
Garb	Glib		
Gas	Glue		
Gate	Goal		
Gay	Goat		
Gear	Gold		
Gem	Golf		

Giraffe

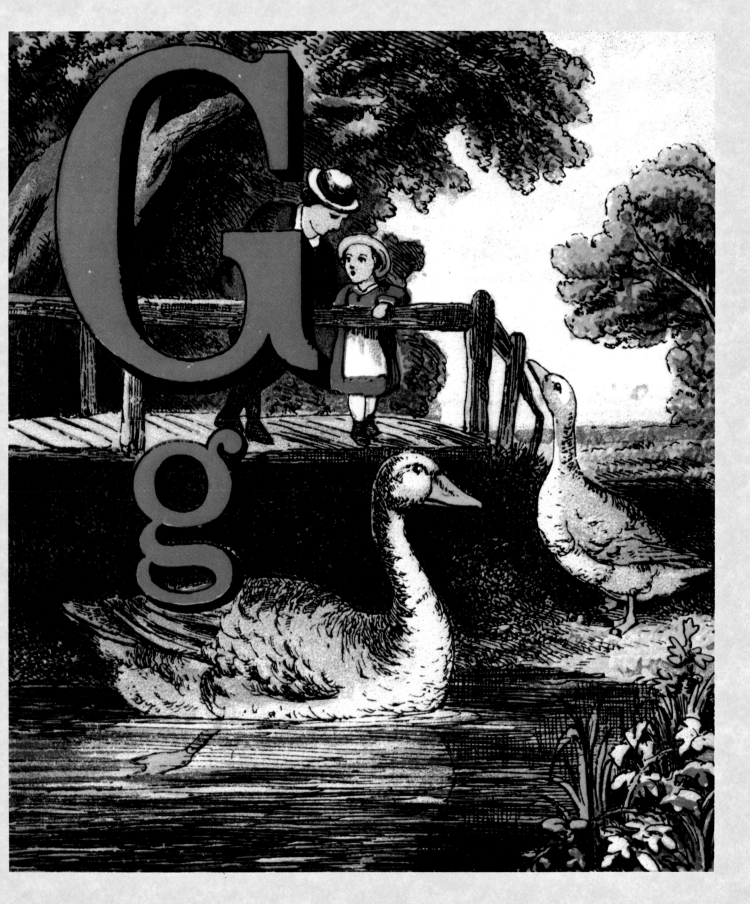

G for the Goose that swims on the pond

Hall	Harp	Help	Hob
Halt	Hat	Hero	Hoe
Ham	Hawk	Hill	Hog
Hand	Hay	Hind	Home
Hang	Head	Hip	Hoof
Hare	Heal	His	Hook
Hark	Heat	Hit	Hoop
Harm	Heel	Hive	Horn

Hedgehog

H for the Hen, of her chickens so fond

E e F f G g H h

E Engine (Fire-engine).   F Fog.

G Guns.   H Horse-Guards.

E e F f G g

H h I i

E Eggs.   F Farm.   G Gate.

H Horses.   I Inn.

I is an Innkeeper, with flagon of ale,
Which **J** the Joiner will drink without
    fail

K a Knife-grinder, sharpens all kinds
    of blades
Razors, scissors and tools for all trades

L a Lamplighter, nimbly skips up and
    down,
And lights in a twinkling the lamps of
    the town

M is a Milkmaid, whose heart is as light
As her milk is pure and her cans are
    bright

Icon	Ink	Jab	Jink
Idea	Inn	Jack	Job
Idle	Iris	Jade	Jog
Idol	Iron	Jail	Join
Ill	Itch	Jam	Joke
Inch	Item	Jape	Jot

Iguana

		Jar	Joy
		Jaw	Jug
		Jay	Jump
		Jest	Junk
		Jet	Just
		Jig	Jut

I for the Icicle, frosty and cold

J for the Jackdaw, perky and bold

Keel   Keg   Key   Kiln

Keen   Kick   Kin

Keep   Kid   Kind

                    Kill   King

Kink

Kiss

Kit

Kite

Kiwi

Knee

Knot

Know

Kangaroo

K for the Kitten that plays with its tail

Lion

Long
Look
Loop
Loot
Lop
Lord

Lace	Leg	Lip	Loss
Lad	Lid	Load	Lost
Lady	Life	Loaf	Love
Lair	Limb	Loam	Low
Lake	Line	Lock	Lure
Lamb	Link	Log	Lyre

L for the Letter that comes by the mail

Man	Maze	Miss	Mood
Map	Meal	Mist	Moon
Mar	Meat	Mix	Moor
Mark	Mend	Moat	More
Mask	Mile	Mob	Moss
Mass	Milk	Mock	Moth
Mast	Mill	Mole	Mud
Mat	Mink	Monk	Mug

Mouse

M for the Monkey, a comical thing

I i J j

I Idlers.   J Jail.

K k L l

K King William's Statue.

L Lamplighter

J j

K k

L l

M m

J Jackdaws.   K Kite.

L Ladder.   M Mill.

N is a Newsboy, who plies well with his
   calling
And "Latest Edition" always is bawling

O an Organ-man, plays tunes grave and
   gay
Content for his pains with very small
   pay

P is a Postman, whose rat-tat so smart
Causes sorrow and joy in many a heart

Q a Quarryman, splits up a mass
Of marble or granite as though it were
   glass

Net	Oat	Peg	
New	Odd	Pen	Owl
Newt	Ode	Pet	
Nib	Oft	Pin	
Nine	Oil	Pit	
Nose	Old	Play	
Note	One	Ply	Quid
Nut	Open	Pond	Quiet
			Quill
			Quire
		Pig	Quit
			Quite

N for the Newsboy, whose cries loudly ring

M m

M Monument.

N n

N News-Boy.

O o

O Omnibus.

P Punch.

P p

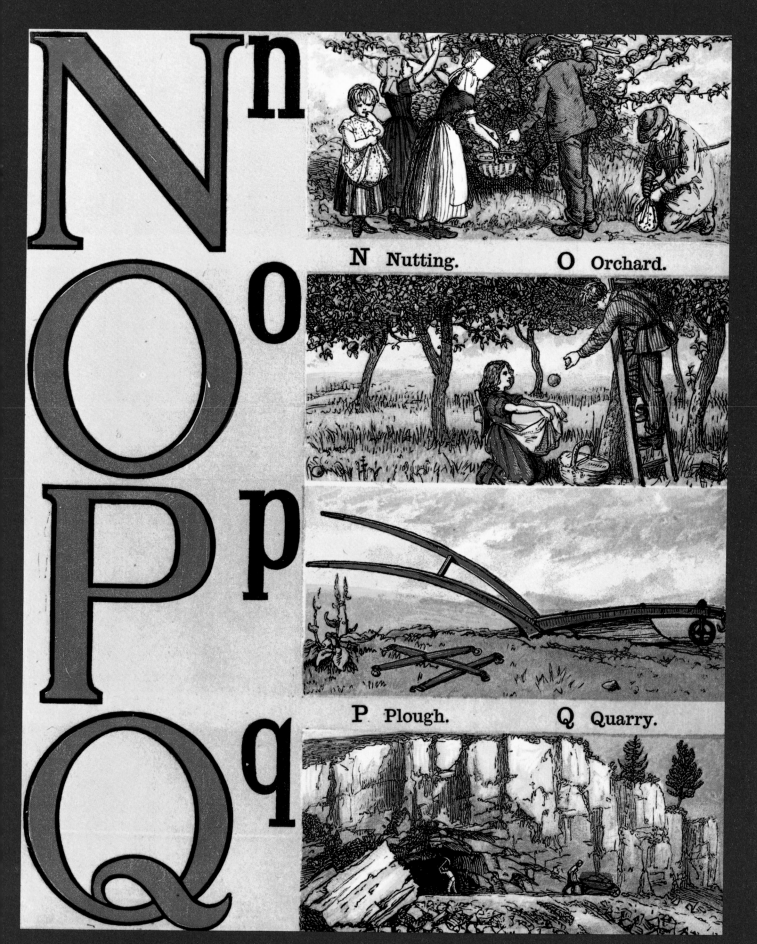

N   Nutting.   O   Orchard.

P   Plough.   Q   Quarry.

R is a Reaper, before whose keen blade
Falls the ripe corn God's goodness has
    made

S is a Shrimper, who gleans from the
    sea
The shrimps and the prawns that give
    zest to our tea

T is a Tinker, who, when holes are
    found
In old pots or kettles, will soon make
    them sound

V is a Verger, courteous and grave,
Who points out the tombs of the pious
    and brave

Red	Saw	Tail	Urn
Rib	Sea	Tale	Use
Rich	Ship	Tap	Vain
Rig	Side	Tart	Vale
Rim		Tea	Van
Ring		Tide	Vane
Rip		Tie	Vary
Road			
Rope			
Row			
Rub			
Run			

Stag

T for the Tinker who mends pots and pans

Q q
R r
S s
T t

Q Queen.   R River.

S Steamer.   T Tower.

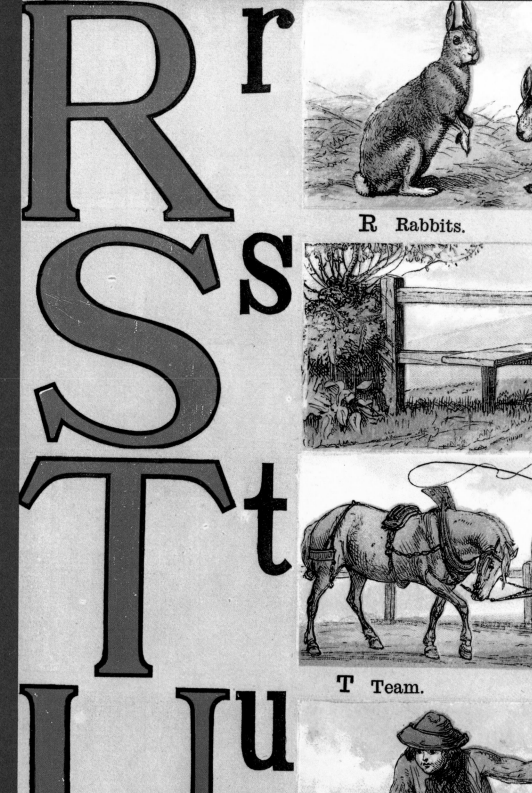

R r
S s
T t
U u

R Rabbits.   S Stile.

T Team.   U Urchin.

W a Washerwoman, always is seen
At her tub, hard at work, rubbing dirty
   things clean

X stands for excellent when on barrels
   of beer,
So the more Xs, the better the beer

Y is a Yeoman, whose fields are well
   till'd,
His men are well housed and his barns
   are well fill'd

Z stands for Zoologist, also for Zany;
So please take your choice, that's if you
   have any

Warm

Warp

Wax

Web

Wed

Weed

Well

Zebra

Wend	Word	Year	Zero
West	Work	Yew	Zest
Wet	Wry	Yoke	Zinc
Whim	Yard	You	Zone
Whip	Yarn	Yule	Zoo

Y for the Yeoman who farms the lands

U u
V v
v Volunteer.
W w
X x
Y y
Z z

U Underground Railway.

W Westminster.

X Y Policemen's No.

Z Zoological Gardens.

V V Vine.   W W Waggon.

Y Y Yew-tree.   Z Zig-zag.